Lou the Crocodile

COLLINGWOOD O'HARE ENTERTAINMENT LTD
Created by Trevor Ricketts and Christopher O'Hare
Series developed by Tony Collingwood
Copyright © 2000 by Collingwood O'Hare Entertainment Ltd.

First published in Great Britain in 2000 by HarperCollins*Children's Books*,
a division of HarperCollins*Publishers* Ltd,
77-85 Fulham Palace Road, Hammersmith, London W6 8JB.
ISBN: 0 00 664749 9
3 5 7 9 10 8 6 4 2
A CIP catalogue record for this title is available from the British Library.

The HarperCollins website address is:
www.fireandwater.com

Printed and bound in Hong Kong.

ANIMAL
STORIES

Lou the Crocodile

Written by Trevor Ricketts

Collins
An Imprint of HarperCollinsPublishers

Crocodile Lou
Was scaly and green,
With rows of sharp teeth
That made her look mean.

Whenever she smiled,
All the animals hid.
"You look a bit scary,"
Said the Monkey called Sid.

What a to do!
She was really quite nice.
But the sight of her teeth
Would frighten the Mice.

She even scared Lion,
Who was usually brave.
And the Bear was so worried
He stayed in his cave.

Poor Lou was sad.
But what could she do?
She went for a walk
And met a Gnu.

Politely she smiled.
The Gnu just stared.
His knees started knocking,
And he begged to be spared.

A few moments later,
During her walk,
She met a green Parrot
Who enjoyed a good talk.

But one smile from Lou
Made his feathers drop out!
He was ever so frightened,
Of that there's no doubt!

Next, she met Snake,
Beneath a big tree.
She stopped for a chat,
He was drinking some tea.

She asked him politely,
"Please may I join you?"
He said, "But of course!
Is it one lump or two?"

They talked for a while,
And ate strawberry cake.
She told him her name.
He said, "My name is Jake."

She couldn't believe it!
He didn't seem scared.
They carried on chatting,
Some biscuits were shared.

After they'd talked
For an hour or two,
Jake showed her his card,
Saying, "This is for you."

"Oh! What is this?"
Said Lou in surprise.
And then, when she read it,
Tears welled in her eyes.

"Can it be true?"
Said Lou to the Snake.
"You're in motion pictures?
It's not a mistake?"

"Indeed it is true,"
Answered young Jake.
"And a star of you
I will certainly make."

A movie was made
In a week and a bit.
It featured a 'Thing',
Whose name was just 'It'.

Lou played this 'Thing',
Which came from beneath.
It crushed little cars,
And chomped its big teeth.

Animals travelled
From far and near.
They all stood in line
From here, to here.

The film, although scary,
Was a massive big hit.
And when Lou chomped her teeth,
It was their favourite bit.

Lou's name was in lights!
Snake had made her a star!
She bought a large house,
And a big shiny car.

She's making a new film –
Part two of part one.
It's called 'Son of It'.
It's really quite fun.

And when she comes home,
She bathes in goats' milk.
Then flops into bed,
Onto pillows of silk.

So Crocodile Lou,
All scaly and green,
Is now a big star
Of the silvery screen.

Now, when she smiles,
All the animals cheer.
She's loved by them all.
She's the 'It' of the year.

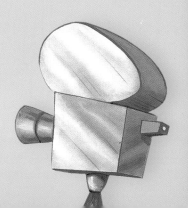

The End